Are We There Yet?

COOL CAR 1

by Mariel Emmerson

Are We There Yet?
© 2022 North Parade Publishing,
Written by Mariel Emmerson

Published by North Parade Publishing, 3-6 Henrietta Mews, Bath BA2 6LR, United Kingdom

Are We There Yet?

by Mariel Emmerson

"We've only just **begun**," said Dad,
"Why don't you play I-Spy?"

"Are we there yet?" Molly yawned, As they left the town **behind**.

"Just look outside the **window**, Mol,
And see what you can **find**."

"Are we there yet?" Harry moaned,
As a bridge loomed up **ahead.**

TROLL
BRIDGE

"Oh, what a massive **rock!**" cried Mum.

"It's **not** a rock!" Mol said.

"Are we there yet?" muttered Mol,

As they passed by a hill.

"Rapunzel's **tower**," Harry spied, "Oh isn't that just **brill!**"

"Are we there yet?"
Harry groaned,

BIG BAD WOLF

As through the woods they **sped.**

"The wolf is baking **cakes!**" cried Mol.
"That sounds like **fun,**" Dad said.

"Are we there yet?" grumbled Mol,

"Just look there!" Harry squealed.

"There's seven dwarves right over there, playing **football** in the **field!**"

"A biscuit's on the move!" whooped Mol.
Mum gave them both a stare.

"It reaches right up to the **sky**!"

"That's **nice**, dear," Mum replied.

COOL CAR 1

"Are we there yet?"
Harry quizzed,

"Are we there yet?" they both cheered.

"Yes!"

laughed Mum and Dad.

"It's gone by very **fast**, you see.

The End

If I Had
A Hundred
Mummies

Written and illustrated
by
Vanda Carter

If I had a hundred mummies
they would have to form a queue
to give me goodnight kisses,
blow my nose and tie my shoes.

We would have to build a bigger house
A multi-storey block of flats
Because mummies have a lot of junk
like motorbikes and hats...

...and frisbees, shoes and pot plants,
coloured fish and smelly cats
and heaps of clothes they never wear
because they got too fat

and when we go on holiday
to Rockpool-on-the-Knose,
you'd better stay at home that day –
there'll be gridlock on the roads

And probably in the sky too!

When my mummies reach the seaside
the beach will soon be packed
with their towels and books and picnics
parasols and paperbacks...

If I had a hundred mummies
keeping eagle-eyes on me
whenever I was naughty
I just know someone would see.

They might make me have a hundred baths
and eat organic Brussels sprouts
and brush my hair each morning
and get cross and shriek and shout.

And they would all be really bossy
and talk about me on the phone
and smother me with kisses
and tell me off and moan...

...and the house would be so crowded
I'd never be alone

Their birthdays would be a nightmare.
A hundred cakes to bake!
And a hundred home-made Mother's Day cards
would take at least a year to make.

Maybe they could share?

No, mummies don't like sharing.

If I had a hundred mummies...

Hang on a minute!

I thought it was a good idea
but now I think it's not.
I DON'T want a hundred mummies,
I'll just have the two I've got!